The Usborne

TREASURY
of ANIMAL
STORIES

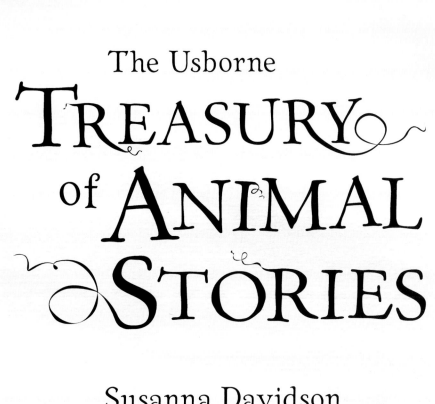

The Usborne
TREASURY
of ANIMAL
STORIES

Susanna Davidson

Illustrated by Rocío Martínez

Designed by Mary Cartwright
and Jessica Johnson

Cover design by Nicola Butler

Contents

Where Stories Come From

A very long time ago, in the vast grasslands of Africa, lived a herd of elephants. Their leader was a wise old elephant, called Themba, who watched over the rest of her herd, from the young mothers to the baby calves, who stumbled around on their newfound legs.

The elephants spent their days roaming the land in search of food – pulling down branches of trees with their long, strong trunks and blowing bubbles in the muddy waterholes. But, as the sun sank low and dusk drew in, the elephants would huddle together under the towering branches of a baobab tree... and beg Themba to tell them a story.

"Grandmama!" the little calves would cry.
"We want stories. Tell us some stories, please."
Then Themba would think and think, swishing her trunk
from side to side as she searched her mind for stories.
But it was of no use. She had nothing to tell.
She listened to the wind. Was the breeze that rustled
through the baobab's leaves trying to tell her a story?
No, there was nothing…no stories…no magical tales.

So one day Themba turned to her younger sister Sipho,
and told her that she must go in search of stories. With a wave
of her trunk, Sipho set out alone across that wide, wide land.
As she walked, she asked everyone she passed if they
could tell her a story.
"I have a hundred stories to tell you," boasted Nogwaja,
the hare. "No, not hundreds, but thousands – millions!"
he added, leaping up and down in the air.
"Oh please," begged Sipho, "give me some,
so that we can tell stories under the trees at night."
"Ummm…" said Nogwaja, twitching his whiskers.
"Actually, I have no time for stories now.
Can't you see that I'm busy?"
"Silly Nogwaja," thought Sipho, sadly.
"He's lying of course. He has no stories."

With a sigh, Sipho went on her way. Night fell,
and Sipho walked on, feeling her way with her sensitive trunk.
"Does anyone know any stories?"
Sipho cried out into the darkness.
"Whoo, hoo, hoo!" replied an owl. "Ask the fish eagle.
He flies higher and sees further than any other bird.
He'll know where you can find stories."

So Sipho followed the river to the sea,
in search of the great fish eagle.
She saw him swooping above the water,
a fish flapping in his claws.
"Nkwazi!" Sipho cried excitedly,
running to the shore.
She so startled the eagle, he dropped
the fish SPLASH! back into the water.
The eagle soared over to Sipho, circling around her, calling out,
"What is so important that you make me lose my supper?"
"Oh great and wise Nkwazi," said Sipho,
"my herd is hungry for stories.
Do you know where I might find some?"
"I am very wise," agreed the fish eagle,
"but I only know of things on the face of the earth.
There is one who knows the secrets of the ocean.
Perhaps he can help you. Wait here and I will call him for you."

8

Sipho waited many days by the raging waves,
until at last, the fish eagle returned. "My friend, the sea turtle
will take you deep deep down, to the place where you can find
stories," he told her. And with that, the great sea turtle lifted
himself out of the ocean.

"Take hold of my tail with the tip of your trunk,"
said the sea turtle, in his deep rumbling voice.
"I will guide you to the land of the Spirit People."

So Sipho took hold of the sea turtle's tail and they went
down to the depths of the sea.

The elephant gazed around her at fish flashing
their shimmering scales. She swam through seaweed forests,
down, down, down, to the land where the Spirit People lived.

The sea turtle took her straight to the thrones of the king
and queen and Sipho bowed before them.

"What do you want from us, creature
from dry lands?" they asked.

9

Sipho told them of her herd, how they gathered
together at dusk but had no stories to share.

"Yes," said the king and queen.

"We have many stories. But what can you give us in return?"

"What do you desire?" asked Sipho.

"We want to hear about life on dry land," they replied.

So Sipho began with the story of her life.

She described the joy of wallowing in mud, the beating sun and
the sound of animals, crying out in the stillness of night.

"You already have the art of telling stories,"
said the king and queen. "You have woven a spell with your
words and carried down to us an image of life in the sun.
In return we give you this shell. Whenever you want a story,
just hold it to your ear and it will tell you a tale."

"Thank you," said Sipho,
bowing before them again.
Then she swam up, up, up, back
to the light and her own dry world.

When she reached the shore,
she walked all those miles back to
her herd, following their scent with
her trunk. And that night, under the
towering branches of a baobab tree, they said,
"Tell us a story, Sipho! Tell us a story."

So Sipho put the shell to her ear, and began,
"Once upon a time..."
And that is how stories came to be.

The Largest Frog There Ever Was

Long, long ago, in the Dreamtime, lived the largest frog there ever was. His name was Tiddalik.

One morning he woke with a terrible thirst.

"Arrrgh!" he croaked. "My throat is parched.

I must drink." So he did.

Tiddalik slurped up water from the frothy springs.
He gurgled and guzzled the burbling streams.
He drank every last drop from the billabongs and bogs
and drained the rivers and lakes.

Then he smacked his lips and croaked,

"I'm STILL thirsty!

There must be more water left in this world."

He searched the sky for rainclouds
with great flicks from his long slimy tongue.
He burst the clouds inside his mouth,
so the raindrops drizzled
down his yawning throat...
    until, at last,
        he was fit to burst.

Tiddalik was finally full.
But without water, the world withered...
The ground cracked. Plants wilted, turned yellow and died.
Leaves dropped from the trees, the trees dropped to
the ground, which heaved a sigh, and said,
"Help, I am dying of thirst."

So all the animals came together
by the dried up banks of the Molonglo River,
to see if they could save the world.

The crocodile spoke first.
"Tiddalik must give us back our water!"
he demanded with a snap.
"But how?" chanted the emu
and the kangaroo.

"We must make Tiddalik laugh!" said a wise old wombat.
"If he will only open his mouth, the water will
come gushing out..."

So the animals rushed to Tiddalik's resting place
down in the Kwongan Sands. The kookaburra kicked
off with his very best joke and the emu
laughed so loudly the wattled bats woke.
But Tiddalik took no notice.
The kangaroo and the wallaroo jumped
through hoops while the blue-tongued skink
turned her tongue to pink.
"What a hoot!"
laughed the rabbit-eared bandicoot.
But Tiddalik took no notice.

For days the animals joked and danced, and sang and
pranced, without a glimmer of a smile from the swollen frog.

And then, at last, the eel slunk onto the scene.

He had been hiding under the last of the mud,
but the baking sun had turned it to dust.
He twirled around. He jumped up and down.

He wriggled and squirmed, then fell flat on the ground.
And for the very first time, Tiddalik forgot to frown and his
lips curved up in a smile.

"More!" cried the wise old wombat.

"Keep going, Mr. Eel, keep going!"
The eel leaped up again and wobbled his body,
while Tiddalik's smile spread over his face and his bulging
cheeks began to shake.

For his final act, the eel stood on one spot, then moved
faster and faster, tying himself in a series of knots.

As Tiddalik watched the writhing eel,
he knew he could stand it no more. He clutched his stomach
and rolled his eyes and let out a huge guffaw.
   The water gushed out from his gaping mouth with
a deafening, thunderous ROAR.
It seeped into the cracks in the dried-up ground,
      then bubbled back up in the springs.
It poured from there into babbling streams,
      which flowed into rivers, which fed the lakes,
         until the world was awash with water once more.
The sky grew darker, the clouds grew bigger, until one by one
 they burst. Then down it came, great buckets of rain,
   bringing life to the land at last.
      Tiddalik looked on in shame.
"I promise," he croaked,
   "never to be so greedy again."

Brer Rabbit
and the Tug of War

Brer Rabbit was bouncing
down the path –
lippity - loppitty,
lippity - loppitty.
He didn't know where he was
going or what he was doing.
He just knew that he was bored.
"It's time I had some fun,"
he decided.

Then, out the corner of his mischief-making eyes,
he spied grumpy Old Rhinoceros, down in a dusty ditch.
He was busy rubbing his wrinkly back on a rock.

"That rhino never shows me any respect," thought Brer
Rabbit, peering down at him.
"Just because I'm a little bit smaller and a little bit younger,
he thinks he can ignore me..."

Then, out the corner of his other
eye, he spied Lady Hippopotamus,
wallowing her roly-poly body
in the gloopy mud.
Brer Rabbit twitched
his whiskers and sniffed.

"As for that hippopotamus…"
he said. "She's as snooty as she is wide."

At that moment, Brer Rabbit
stopped bouncing and started
thinking. Dangling from the branch
above him was a twisty, ropy old vine.

"Ho, ho, ho!" said Brer Rabbit. "I know
how I can have some fun." He pulled at that ropy
old vine until finally he pulled it free. Then he picked it
up in his paws and

lippity - loppitty,

lippity - loppitty

he bounced with it down to the ditch.

"Wrinkly Rhinoceros!" called Brer Rabbit. "You're about
as old as that rock there, aren't you? I could beat you,
paws down, in a tug of war. You wouldn't stand a chance
against bold and brainy Brer Rabbit."

"Pipsqueak!" grunted Old Rhinoceros.
"You might be bold and brainy but you
sure aren't brawny. Give me that vine
and I'll show you how strong I am."

"If you're sure," said Brer
Rabbit. "Now, you just stay there,
Wrinkly Rhino. I'm going around
the hill. Wait until you feel me
pull my end of the vine,
then we'll begin."

Quick as a flash, Brer Rabbit bobbed over to the
wallowing hippo. "Laaa-zy Hippopotamus!" he called.
"Don't you do anything but lie around in mud all day?
I bet my ears and whiskers I could beat you in a tug of war.
You wouldn't stand a chance against
the brave and brilliant Brer Rabbit."
Lady Hippopotamus blew a series of bubbles through
her nose, to show her disgust.
"How dare you talk to me like that,
you good-for-nothing ball of fluff.
Give me that vine and I'll show you how strong I am."
Brer Rabbit handed it over and bounded back
the way he'd come. "Wait there!" he called.
"When I pull my end, we'll begin."
Brer Rabbit hopped until he
was halfway between them.

Then, with a chuckle of pure glee, he pulled once to the left, and once to the right.

Not expecting Brer Rabbit to put up much of a fight, the two great beasts responded with a careless tug.

Neither of them budged.

"Hmm," said Old Rhinoceros. "Well this should do it," and he pulled with all his might.

"Whoah!" cried Lady Hippopotamus, as she was dragged through the mud. "Heave-ho!" she hollered, straining back with a tremendous tug.

Old Rhinoceros and Lady Hippopotamus kept on pulling
and tugging and tugging and pulling until their flanks heaved
and they were weak at the knees.

"Really, that rabbit is amazing!"
panted Lady Hippopotamus.
"He's stupendous!"
puffed Old Rhinoceros.

Sitting on a hill, watching them
both, Brer Rabbit laughed
and laughed until
he could laugh no more.
Then he got a little saw
and cut the vine in two.
SPLASH!
Lady Hippopotamus flew back into the mud.

SPLAT! Old Rhinoceros landed flat on his wrinkly
back. When Lady Hippopotamus looked up,
Brer Rabbit was standing over her, a twinkle in his eye.
"The vine broke! Shall I find another,
so we can start again?"
"No, no!" said the heaving hippo.
She watched Brer Rabbit leaping around
and let out a heartfelt sigh. "You're
stronger than me. How can that be?"

"You shouldn't judge by appearances," said Brer Rabbit. "Everything isn't always as it seems."

"Oh ho ho! Old Rhino!" Brer Rabbit called next, leaping over to the dusty ditch. "The vine broke.
But here's a new one so we can start again."
Old Rhinoceros shuddered. "That's enough for me," he said. "You're... a... mighty strong rabbit, you know."

From that day, Lady Hippopotamus and Old Rhinoceros treated Brer Rabbit with the utmost respect.
"Great Brer Rabbit!" they called, whenever he bobbed by. And Brer Rabbit would hold his head high and think,
"Oh! How bold and brave and brilliant am I!"

How Bear Lost his Tail

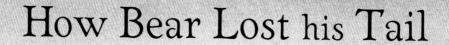

In the days when animals could talk,
Bear had a long, sleek and shapely tail.
"It's the most beautiful tail in the world,"
 boasted Bear, and he waved it in the air for all to see.
 "I bet you wished you had a tail like mine,"
Bear told Snake.

"Yesss," hissed Snake, and slithered away.
 "I bet you wish you had a tail like mine,"
Bear told Chipmunk.

"Yes," squeaked Chipmunk, and scurried away.
 "I bet you wish you had a tail like mine," Bear told Fox.

"No," said Fox, who was fed up with Bear boasting about
his tail. Secretly, Fox thought it was time someone
played a trick on Bear. "He's far too pleased
with himself," Fox thought. "And seeing
as I'm the best trickster in the land,
it had better be me…"

It was the time of year when
Hatho, the Spirit of Frost, swept
across the land. So the lakes were
covered with ice, the trees were coated
in shining white snowflakes and there
was little food around.

Fox knew that Bear would be very hungry
and he used this as part of his plan. He made a hole in the ice,
just where Bear liked to walk. When Bear came lumbering by,
he found Fox sitting with his tail dangling through the ice,
surrounded by a ring of glistening fish.
"Greetings, Brother," said Bear.
"What are you doing?"
"Greetings," replied Fox. "I'm fishing.
Would you like to try?"

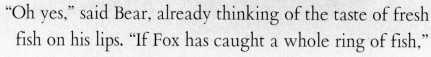

"Oh yes," said Bear, already thinking of the taste of fresh
fish on his lips. "If Fox has caught a whole ring of fish,"
he thought, "how many will I catch? After all,
my tail is longer and stronger than Fox's."
"We must find a new hole for you,"
said Fox. "I have already caught all
the fish in this part of the river."
And he took Bear to a shallow lake,
where Fox knew there were
no fish at all.
Fox made a hole in the ice for Bear.
"Now," he said, "you must do as I tell you.
Turn your back to the hole and place your
tail inside it. When a fish bites, pull your tail
out as fast as you can. But don't move until you've
caught a fish, or you'll scare them all away."

26

"Just this once, I will do exactly as you say," said Bear. And he placed his treasured tail in the icy water.

Fox watched Bear to make sure he did just what he told him, then he crept back to his underground house and went to bed.

That night, snow fell in thick drifts. When Fox stuck his nose out of the earth the next morning, he saw that the whole world was white.

"I should go and check on Bear," he thought. "I wonder if he's still there?"

Fox padded down to the lake, but he couldn't see Bear anywhere. Then, from the middle of the lake, he heard a series of loud snores. They were coming from a huge white mound in the middle of the ice.

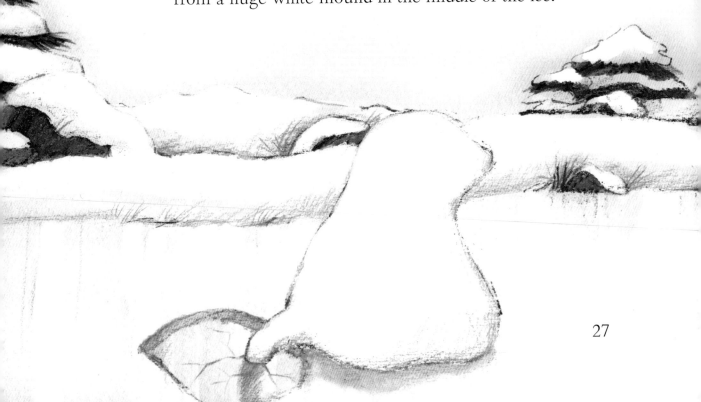

27

"That's Bear, covered in snow!" Fox realized,
and he had to muffle his mouth with his tail, to stop himself
from laughing out loud.

"It's time to wake him up!" Fox decided.

He crept right up to Bear's ear,

took a deep breath and barked,

"Now Bear!"

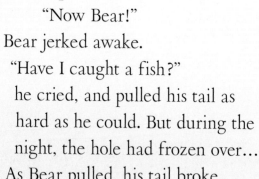

Bear jerked awake.

"Have I caught a fish?"

he cried, and pulled his tail as

hard as he could. But during the

night, the hole had frozen over...

As Bear pulled, his tail broke

off with a SNAP!

Just like that.

Bear turned around, hoping to see a
juicy trout. Instead he saw his long, sleek and shapely tail,
lying forlornly on the ice.

"Fox!" cried Bear. "I'll get you for this."

But even though Fox was laughing, he was
still faster than Bear. He leaped into the forest
and raced away, in a blur of glossy red fur.

So it is to this day that Bears
have short tails and no love for Foxes.

The Lion and the Mouse

The mouse scurried across the grassy plain. Every time he heard a noise, he stopped, stared and pricked up his ears. He knew there was danger in every direction – from hawks in the sky above, to snakes on the ground below...

The mouse was so worried, he didn't stop to think about the large, golden hill in front of him. If he had, he would have noticed how it was moving gently up and down

and making deep, rumbly purring noises.

But as it was, he ran up it, his feet pitter-pattering over the soft, moving mound. Up and up and up he went...

...then WOOOSH! down the other side.

"Ooh my!" he muttered.
"What a slippery hill this is."

Before he knew it, the mouse was tumbling
head-over-paws down the silky smooth slope.
He went tumble-bounce, tumble-bounce, tumble-bounce,
until he landed with a BUMP on a cold, wet, black... nose.

"How strange," said the mouse. "I've never met a
hill with a nose before."

Two huge eyes blinked open. "I'M NOT A HILL,"
said a booming voice. "I'M A VERY ANGRY LION.

How dare you wake me up!" And with that, the lion snatched
up the mouse in his claws.

The mouse gulped. "I'm so sorry,"
he whispered. "So very, very sorry."

"Do you know what I do to those who
wake me?" the lion went on.

The terrified little mouse shook his head.
"I eat them up," said the lion.

"All it'll take with you is
one quick SNAP."

"Oh please," said the
mouse. "Don't eat me. I'm so
small, I'd make such a tiny

morsel. I wouldn't fill you up at all. Just think, if you spare my life today, maybe one day I'll save yours!"

The lion opened his mouth wide.
The mouse saw rows of gleaming white dagger-sharp teeth and a fiery red tongue. He bowed his head
and waited for the lion's bite to come.

It never did. With a roar of laughter, the lion collapsed on his back, waving his enormous paws in the air.

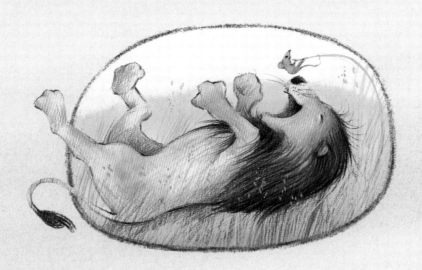

"You save my life!" he laughed. "What a joke!
How could a mouse ever help the mighty King of the Beasts? Be off with you, my little friend.
You've made me laugh enough for a week."

The mouse didn't wait for the lion to stop laughing.
He hurried away as fast as his legs could take him.

A week later, the lion was coming out of his lair when he walked across a rope and...SNAP!

He was caught in a hunter's trap.
No matter how hard he struggled,
he couldn't break free.
"So I just have to wait here for the hunters
to come," thought the lion. "How could
this have happened to ME?
I'm King of the Beasts!"
And he roared and roared in anger.
Far away, on the other side of
the plains, the little mouse heard
the lion's cries.
"He's in trouble," he thought.
"I must help him."
Without a moment's delay,
the mouse scurried out to
the lion's lair, where he
found him roaring and
gnashing in a mesh of ropes.
"Don't worry, lion,"
squeaked the mouse.
"I'm here to help."
"What can you do, little mouse?"
scoffed the lion, while tears of rage poured down his face.
"It's too late to save me. I'm trapped for good."
"Shh!" ordered the mouse. "Keep still."
The mouse began to gnaw.

He worked as fast as he could, but the
ropes were thick and his teeth were small.
The sun went down, the sky grew
dark and the stars came out – and still the
little mouse gnawed and gnawed. But by
sunrise the next morning, the lion
was finally free.

He stepped out of the net, arched his back, threw back
his head and let out a tremendous ROAR. Standing
there, his great mane lit up by the rising sun, the
little mouse shook to see how big he was.
"Thank you," said the lion, looking
down at the mouse. "You saved my life.
I was wrong to laugh at you.
I see little friends can be
great friends, after all."

The Monkey and the Crocodile

Down by the banks of the Ganges River, stood a beautiful rose-apple tree. In among its branches, lived a sleek and golden monkey. He loved nothing more than to laze in its shade and dine on its succulent fruit.

One sunny day, the monkey saw a great long crocodile crawl out of the water and rest on the bank below.

"Try one of these," called the monkey, tossing down the rosy ripe fruit. "It's the most delicious food in the world."

The crocodile caught the fruit in his toothy jaws. "Mmm," he said, as he chomped it down. "How perfectly scrumptious. So sweet! So juicy! Thank you, my friend."

After that, the crocodile visited the monkey every day.

Together, they would eat the fruit of that wonderful tree and talk in its cooling shade.

"Have you a wife?" asked the monkey, one day.

"I do," said the crocodile.

"Then you must take her my very best rose-apples," declared the monkey, "so she too can taste their sweetness."

The crocodile opened up his enormous jaws,
and the monkey filled his friend's mouth with fruit.
The crocodile's wife was overjoyed.
"Oh how delectable!" she cried, gulping the rose-apples down.
"Where did you get them?"

"From a tree on the banks of the Ganges,"
the crocodile replied.

"But you can't climb trees," pointed out his wife.
"Did you collect them from the ground?"

"Oh no! My friend the monkey throws them down
for me to eat. Then we talk together in the shade."

"So that's why you're so late home these days," said his
wife. "Ooh," she went on, licking her jaws. "A monkey that
lives off rose-apples must have such sweet flesh. I bet his heart
tastes like heaven. Bring it to me!"

"I can't," cried the crocodile, quite appalled.
"The monkey is my friend."

"BRING IT TO ME," snapped his wife.
"Or I shall starve myself to death."

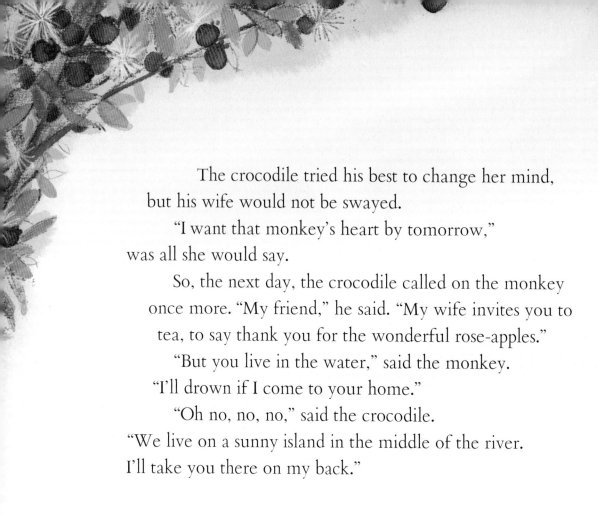

The crocodile tried his best to change her mind,
but his wife would not be swayed.

"I want that monkey's heart by tomorrow,"
was all she would say.

So, the next day, the crocodile called on the monkey
once more. "My friend," he said. "My wife invites you to
tea, to say thank you for the wonderful rose-apples."

"But you live in the water," said the monkey.
"I'll drown if I come to your home."

"Oh no, no, no," said the crocodile.
"We live on a sunny island in the middle of the river.
I'll take you there on my back."

The monkey climbed down from his rose-apple tree, his arms full of fruit for the crocodile's wife. He leaped onto his friend's slippery back and with a splish and a splash they were off, crossing the wide, wide river.

The nearer they came to the crocodile's home, the worse the crocodile felt. "The monkey is my friend," he thought. "I don't want my wife to eat him."

At last he could take it no more. "I haven't been quite straight with you, my friend," he said. "My wife has invited you to tea only because she wants to eat your heart."

"Eat my heart?" cried the monkey, thinking fast. "Is that what she wants? Why didn't you tell me before? I don't keep my heart with me, my friend. It's far too precious for that. It's safely stored at the top of my tree."

"Then let us go back and get it," said the crocodile.
And the monkey happily agreed.

    With a swish of his tail, the crocodile turned around
and headed back for the opposite bank.
    As soon as they touched dry land, the monkey sprang
off the crocodile's back, rushed up his tree...
    and didn't come down.
    "What are you doing?" asked the crocodile, waiting
patiently on the ground.
    "Didn't you know we monkeys carry our hearts within us?"
said the monkey. "My foolish friend! Go away,
        and tell your wife, I'm never giving either
           of you a rose-apple again."

Brer Rabbit gets his Comeuppance

One sunny day, Brer Rabbit was bouncing along –
lippety - loppitty, lippety - loppitty –
when he saw Tortoise basking in the sun.

Brer Rabbit flopped down beside him and they lazed
the afternoon away, swapping stories and telling tall tales.

It wasn't long before Brer Rabbit was boasting
as usual. "I'm the fastest runner in the world!" he said.
But Tortoise wasn't having any of it. No sir!

"I bet I can beat you in a race," Tortoise told him.

Brer Rabbit nearly split his sides laughing.
"You creep along so slowly it's hard to tell if you're
even moving," he scoffed. "You'll never beat me, slowcoach."

"Oh yes I will!" said Tortoise, puffing out his chest.

"Meet me tomorrow morning right here. I'll wear a white feather on my head so you can see me in the tall grass. We'll run over those four hills. The first one to reach the top of the fourth hill is the winner."

"You're on," said Brer Rabbit, hopping away.

He was so sure he'd beat Tortoise, he told everyone he knew to come along to the race. "Wait for us at the finishing line," he said. "Of course, I'll be there first."

As soon as Brer Rabbit had gone, Tortoise shuffled off to find his family. "Brer Rabbit is the fastest animal around," he thought to himself. "And what's more, he's tricked everyone in town. Now, how am I going to outwit him…?"

By the time Tortoise had reached his family, he'd worked out a plan. "I'm going to give each of you a white feather," he told them. "I want you to position yourselves at points along the race – at the top of each hill and at the bottom of each valley.

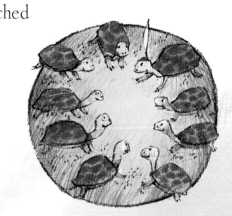

Make sure you
show yourselves when
Brer Rabbit comes by."
The next morning, the two
animals met at the starting point.
"Ready,

steady,

GO!"

cried an excited fox, and they were off.

Brer Rabbit sped away, his bobbing white tail
disappearing into the distance.

Tortoise's brother, wearing his white feather, crawled
along for a little while – plod, plod, plod.

Then, as soon as Brer Rabbit was out of view, he snuck
back into the bushes, a little smile on his wrinkly face.

41

As Brer Rabbit came bounding up the first
hill, he saw Tortoise trudging along ahead of
him. Brer Rabbit was amazed. "I thought I'd
left him for dust!"

The furious rabbit put on a massive burst
of speed and shot ahead of the tortoise.

"Ha ha! Take that!" he cried.

But, as soon as Brer Rabbit had turned his back,
Tortoise's brother took off his white feather and crawled
back into the bushes, chuckling to himself.

When Brer Rabbit reached the valley floor, there was
Tortoise ahead of him again, his white feather plain to see.
"I can't believe it!" cried Brer Rabbit.
"He must have crawled past me."
With a flick of his hind legs, Brer Rabbit bounded
and leaped as fast as he could go.

Once again, he shot past Tortoise,
but every time he reached a hilltop or
came bouncing down into a valley,
Tortoise was always one step ahead,
crawling along without a care in the world.

Brer Rabbit came up the fourth hill.
The view was clear.
"I've done it! I've done it!" he thought,
but at the last moment, Tortoise
appeared again, right by the finishing line.

With an achingly slow lift of his flat front foot,
Tortoise crossed the line.

He was – THE WINNER!

Brer Rabbit flew by him seconds later, in a flash of pale fur.
But it was too late. He had lost the race.

"Three cheers for Tortoise!" cried the crowd.

As Tortoise nodded his head to all his admirers,
Brer Rabbit collapsed, exhausted, in the dust.

"It doesn't look like you're the fastest after all," said Tortoise.

"I still think you're slow-moving," retorted Brer Rabbit,
"but now I know you're quick-witted too. If only I could
work out how you won that race."

Tortoise just smiled. For once,
someone had got the better of Brer Rabbit.

How the Rhinoceros got his Skin

Once upon a time, by the shores of the Red Sea,
there lived a young man named Manee, who wore
a wonderful hat that reflected the rays of the sun.

Manee owned nothing more than his hat, his knife
and his piping hot cooking stove.

One day he took flour and water and currants
and nutmeg and sugar and plums and made himself
an enormous cake, two feet across and three feet thick.
He put it to cook on his piping hot stove, and cooked
it and cooked it until it was golden brown
and smelled most sensational.

But just as he was going to eat it, there
came down to the beach a Rhinoceros.
He had a horn on his nose, two piggy
eyes and very few manners.

In those days the Rhinoceros's
skin fitted him snugly and tightly with
no wrinkles in it anywhere.
All the same he had no manners then
and he has no manners now, and he
never will have any manners.

"GRUNT!" went the Rhinoceros,
and Manee left the cake and shot up
the nearest palm tree.

Then the Rhinoceros tipped over the cooking
stove with the end of his nose and gobbled up the cake.
When he had finished eating he went away, waving his
tail behind him.

Manee came down from his palm tree and put the stove
on its legs and said:

Them that takes cakes
Which the great Manee bakes
Makes dreadful mistakes.

And he meant it.

Five weeks later, there was a heat wave in the Red Sea
and everybody took off all the clothes they had. Manee took off
his hat and the Rhinoceros took off his skin and carried it over
his shoulder as he came down to the beach to bathe. In those
days it buttoned underneath with three buttons, just like a coat.

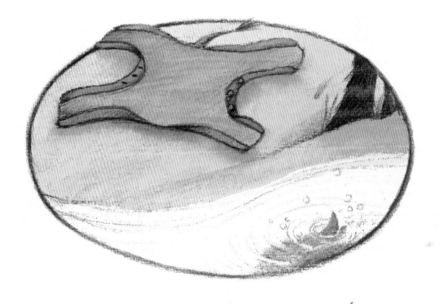

He passed Manee and said nothing at all
about the cake, as he never had any manners then,
now or henceforward. The Rhinoceros waddled straight
into the water and blew bubbles through his nose, leaving his
skin on the beach.

Manee waited until he was sure the Rhinoceros
wasn't watching. Then he rushed to his camp and filled
his hat with cake crumbs. And he took that skin
and he shook that skin...

and he scrubbed that skin...

and he rubbed that skin
full of old, dry, stale, tickly cake crumbs, as much as it could hold.

When he was done,
he climbed to the top of his palm tree
and waited for the Rhinoceros to come
out of the water and put it on.

And the Rhinoceros did.
He buttoned it up with the three buttons
and straight away it began to tickle him.
He wanted to scratch, but it made it worse.
Then he lay down in the sand and rolled
and rolled and every time he rolled the cake
crumbs tickled him worse and worse.

He ran to the palm tree and rubbed
and rubbed himself against it. He rubbed
so hard that he rubbed his skin into a
great fold over his shoulders, and another
fold underneath and he rubbed his
three buttons right off.

Then he rubbed some
more folds into his legs until he was
quite out of temper. But it didn't make
the least difference to the cake crumbs.
They were right inside his skin and OH!
how it tickled.
So the Rhinoceros went home, very angry
and horribly scratchy.
And from that day to this, every rhinoceros
has great folds in his skin and a very bad temper,
on account of the tickly cake crumbs.

Why Dogs and Cats are Enemies

Long ago, in a city in the far-flung north of China, lived an old man and his two friends – a long-limbed dog and a midnight-black cat.

The old man's house was hidden behind high stone walls. No one ever went in, and no one ever came out, and people began to wonder what went on inside.

One evening, when the moon was wrapped in cloud, a thief climbed the walls of the old man's house. He slithered in through an open window and gazed around him in wonder.

Silver lanterns lit a room laden with treasures.
Jade pillars spiralled to the ceiling, gold carvings shimmered in all four corners and exquisite paintings of dragons danced across the walls.
The thief stole through the house,
                                    slipping from shadow to shadow.
Finally he crept into the room where the old man sat, with the dog and cat beside him.
"And what would you like to eat?" the old man asked his dog.

50

The dog barked once and the man laughed.

"I thought so!" he said, drawing from his pocket
a long ivory wand.

"As you like it, as I like it, I would like some tasty beef
stew," he said, tapping the wand.

All at once, a silver bowl brimming with stew appeared
in the air and floated down to the floor. The dog wolfed down
his dinner, wagging his tail.

"And what would you like?" the old man asked the cat,
who was curled in a ball at his feet. The cat merely blinked
her emerald eyes.

"The same as usual, then," he said, tapping his wand
again. This time, a gleaming, pink salmon appeared, and landed
on the table with a slap. The cat began to eat it up, as daintily
as an empress dining in a palace.

The old man tapped his wand a third time.
"Duck and plum sauce and dumplings for me!"
he said. A second later the food appeared, steaming
in golden bowls. After supper, the old man yawned.
Then, one by one, they went to bed,
snuggling down into silken sheets.

The thief crept silently into the old man's bedroom,
took the wand and was gone.

The next morning, the old man woke and reached for
his wand. Finding it missing, he frantically searched his
house, toppling treasures and tearing scrolls as he looked.
"I'm ruined!" he cried. "I'm lost without that wand."
The dog padded up to his side and the old man
looked into the dog's bright, eager eyes and said,
"Will you be my strong legs and find the thief?"
The dog wagged his tail eagerly and barked.
Then the old man turned to his cat.
"Will you be my clever mind and find the thief?" he asked.
The cat purred softly and licked his hand.
Quick as a flash, the two animals raced
out the door to begin their search.

They looked all over China for their master's wand, risking their lives and living by their wits. But the thief was nowhere to be found. Then, at last, they heard of a mysterious man who had appeared from nowhere, with more money than the Emperor himself. He lived in a grand house, surrounded on all sides by a swirling river.

"I'll never make it," said the cat, as they gazed across the torrid waters. "I'm far too weak. You must carry me!"

And she leaped onto the dog's back.

The dog plunged into the water. It was so cold it made him gasp. He strained to keep his head above the surface, but the river swept around him like a thousand icy serpents.

"I can't go on," he panted.

"Come on!" urged the cat. "Think of tasty beef stew, and soft silk sheets!"

The dog thought of his master, far away, and struggled on.

Soon they reached the other side, where they both stopped in their tracks.

The thief was standing outside the house, with the wand dangling from a cord.

"Now!" barked the dog, and he pelted past the startled guards, knocking the thief to the ground.

"HELP!" screamed the thief.

The guards tried to grab hold of the dog, but he sank his teeth deep into the thief's robe.

In a flash of fur, the cat streaked in and gripped the wand between her paws. The thief tried to snatch it back, but she sank her sharp teeth deep into his flesh.

"Aaaayeee!" he yelped.

"As you like, as I like, may I be home again," wished the cat. "Wait for me!" wailed the dog, but the cat had already vanished.

The next moment, the cat was back in the old man's house. It had changed completely. A cold wind whistled through dark, empty rooms, and the old man sat alone, staring at nothing.

As the cat weaved around his ankles, a smile lit up his face.

"You're safe! Thank goodness!" he cried, picking her up and tickling her silk-soft ears.

"I don't care about the wand," he said, "I'm just glad you're home again."

Then looking down, he saw the wand lying at his feet. "You brought it back," he said, stroking the cat on the nose.

"But where's the dog?" the old man asked. "Did he run off and leave you all alone?"

The cat gazed up at the old man with her sad, green eyes, and mewed.

"That cold-hearted scoundrel!" cursed the old man. "My poor, courageous cat," he added, and she settled down snugly onto his lap.

Summer turned to winter, and snow lay thick and heavy on the ground. One night, there was a scratching at the door. The old man opened it, and there, on the doorstep, was his dog. His ear was torn, and he was thin and scraggly as a scarecrow. But he leaped and jumped and barked for joy, delighted to see his master again.

"Oh!" the old man snorted. "Now the cat's returned my fortune, you decided to come back, did you?"

"Tell him what happened!" the dog barked at the cat. But the sly, fat cat simply smiled.

"If you don't stop that yapping," the old man snapped, "I'll wish you from here to the Himalayas!"

And he slammed the door in the dog's face. The dog slunk away through the snow, sorrow in his heart. The cat stayed with her master, and kept him to her sleek, shiny self. But all dogs have remembered the cat's betrayal that day, and have hated cats ever since.

Clever Jackal
Tricks the Lion

"Kwasuka sukela…" this story begins (that means "Once upon a time" in Zulu)… the most cunning animal in all of Africa was trotting along with his nose to the ground. It was, of course, the mischievous, rascally, trickster Jackal. At that moment, he was sniffing around for his next meal. Sniff, sniff, sniff, he went… "Mmm, I smell lizard," he muttered, "that would make a tasty snack. And can I smell antelope too? No, something bigger… something much bigger…"

Clever Jackal lifted his nose and came face-to-face
with... Lion, or Great Bhubesi as he was known in that land.

"Oops," thought Clever Jackal. He had played one
too many tricks on Great Bhubesi, and the snarly old
lion was probably wanting revenge.

In a flash, Clever Jackal thought of a plan.
He cowered at the side of the path, sending
terrified, darting glances at the craggy
rocks above. "Help!" cried Clever Jackal.
"Help! Help!"
Lion stopped in surprise.
"Oh Great Bhubesi," said Clever Jackal.
"There is no time to lose. See those great
rocks above us? They're about to fall!
We'll both be crushed to death.
Do something, mighty lion.
Do something, or we shall
both be killed."

Great Bhubesi looked
up in alarm, while Clever
Jackal cowered even lower
to the ground, putting up
his paws to protect his head.

"Hurry," said Clever Jackal.
"Hurry!"

So Great Bhubesi bounded over and put his strong
shoulder beneath the rock, straining under its weight.

"Thank you, great king," said Clever Jackal.
"I will go and find a log to put under the rock,
so we can hold it up."

And the next moment, Clever Jackal was out of sight.
Five hours later, Great Bhubesi was still standing under the rock.
"Jackal isn't coming back," he realized at last. "GRRRR!"

... and Warthog Tries to Copy Him

A few days later, Warthog was busy making himself a new home. It was inside an old termite mound and wonderfully spacious. Warthog bumbled around, widening the entrance and burrowing away, until it was utterly perfect. He was very pleased with himself. "Even Clever Jackal doesn't have such a good home," Warthog thought to himself. "Mine is the most magnificent house in all of Africa."

Every day, Warthog would stand at the entrance with his snout in the air. He watched lots of giraffes and zebras and wildebeest walking by on their way to the watering hole, and pitied them.

59

"Hah!" he thought. "No one has such a fine home as me."

One day, as Warthog stood proudly outside his new home, his snout tipped skywards, he was horrified to spy Great Bhubesi, the Lion, stalking steathily up to him.

Warthog started to back away, but he had made the entrance to his home so grand and wide, Great Bhubesi would have no trouble following him inside.

"Help!" panicked Warthog. "Bhubesi will eat me in my own home. What can I do?"

Then, with great relief, Warthog remembered the trick Clever Jackal had told him. Why, Jackal had been bragging about it only the other day.

The next moment, Warthog arched his back so it touched the roof of his entrance and cried out, "Help! I am going to be crushed. The roof is caving in. Flee, Great Bhubesi, before you are crushed along with me."
The Great Bhubesi looked down at Warthog and ROARED!

"Do you think I am a fool?" he said. "I remember this trick of Jackal's. I'm not going to be caught out again."

Trembling with fear, Warthog dropped to his knees.
"Oh Great Bhubesi," he cried. "Have mercy on me.
Don't eat me – please!"

"Luckily for you, I'm not hungry," said Great Bhubesi.
"I have just dined on fresh antelope. But from now on, you must stay on your knees, you foolish beast."

Lion laughed to himself and walked away, shaking his shaggy head. "Ha!" he thought. "That slow-witted fool tried to copy Jackal's trick."

As for Warthog... he never forgot the lion's command.
And to this day, you will see him feeding on his knees,
with his bottom in the air and his snout to the ground,
looking very undignified indeed.

The Bird who Could Only Smile

High up in the cloud forests of Colombia, a bushbird was sitting in a bamboo bush, feeling lonely. He called out to the leaping monkeys and glistening frogs,
the slithering snakes and chattering toucans,
but they all passed him by with a smile and a wave.
"Don't you look happy today!" they said. For Bushbird had a problem... his beak curved up in an upturned line so no matter how hard he tried to frown, he could only ever smile.

"I'm NOT happy today!" Bushbird cried.
"I'm lonely!" But no one took any notice.
Bushbird always seemed so happy,
they thought, he didn't need any friends.
So instead Bushbird sat on his branch
and covered his head with his wing.

At last, a little howler monkey stopped by his side
and peered at the sooty bundle of feathers bunched down
on the end of the branch. "Is that you, Bushbird?" he asked.

Under his wing, Bushbird nodded.

"Are you all right?" asked the howler monkey.

Bushbird just stuck his head further under his wing.

"Oh Bushbird!" said the howler monkey. "I've never seen
you like this. Are you feeling sad?"

"I am," croaked Bushbird. "Oh, I am!"

So the little monkey howled as loud as he could.
"Come quick!" he called. "Bushbird is feeling sad."

There was a flurry of wings and a pounding of feet
and the branches shook as the other animals came rushing.

"Poor Bushbird," they said. "Come out from under
your wing. We'll comfort you."

So Bushbird peered out from behind his
feathers to show his beaming, curving smile.

The little howler monkey gasped in surprise.
"You tricked me!" he cried.

"Ha!" cackled a parakeet.
"You're as happy as ever – we can see."

"No... come back!" cried Bushbird,
but the animals turned away.

"There must be a way to show
how lonely I am," thought Bushbird.
And at last, as night fell, he knew how to
do it. As the moon sank down behind the
clouds, Bushbird began to sing.
He sang of lonely days and long dark nights
and the sadness behind his smile.
The monkeys woke and heard his haunting song.
Baby monkeys crept close to their mothers for comfort, and
their mothers hugged them closer still. The frogs' skins
prickled with sadness and even the viper felt tears
sting his eyes. "Who could be singing this
sad, sad song?" they wondered.

And they followed the sound to the
bamboo bush where the bushbird sang
in the dark. But as they gazed up with
pity-filled eyes, the clouds began to
part. A glimmer of moonlight lit up
the bushbird's smile.

"What a horrible trick to play!" cried the
glistening golden frogs.

"Once was funny – twice is too much," huffed
the howler monkeys.

"Look at your gloating smile," added the viper.
"You're as happy as you ever were. Get away!"

So Bushbird flew far, far away. He flew all through that dark night. "I'll live by myself," he decided. "I can't be any lonelier than I am now."

When morning broke, he found himself in the most secret part of the forest. The only sounds were the rustling leaves... and a creature, rooting around on the ground. It had funny pointy feet and a stubby little tail. But strangest of all was its droopy snout that dangled over its chin.

It had the saddest face Bushbird had ever seen.

"Who are you?" asked Bushbird.

"I'm a tapir," the creature replied.

"You look just how I feel!" said Bushbird, gazing at the sorrowful face.

"This is how tapirs always look," the creature replied, "no matter how happy we are. I think you need to look in a creature's eyes to see how they feel inside."

From that day on, the bushbird and the tapir were the best of friends. Each knew exactly how the other felt... even though one always wore a frown, and the other a glorious, curling smile.

The Ant and the Grasshopper

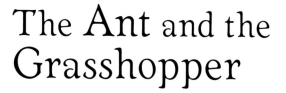

It was a hot summer's day. Bees were buzzing, butterflies were fluttering and a grasshopper was chirping in the grass, singing away to his heart's delight.

"This is the life," he thought, as he swayed around in the wind. He looked up at the blue, blue sky and let out a very contented sigh.

"I don't know how you've got time to laze around all day," muttered a squeaky little voice below him. "There's so much to be done. I don't even have time to stop and catch my breath."

Grasshopper peered down, to see an ant scurrying around beneath him with a plump ear of corn on his back.

"What you need is to relax," chirruped Grasshopper. "Enjoy life! Don't work all the time."

"I'm preparing for winter," said Ant, importantly. "You should do the same."

"Why should I bother about winter?" asked Grasshopper. "It's summer now and I have all the food I need. Besides," he added. "I love to sing."

"You're a fool," said Ant, and scurried on.

Summer passed by in a haze of warm days. Grasshopper's song carried far and wide on the breeze. He leaped above the waving corn crying, "Summer's here!

Summer's here! It's time to play!"

He was having a wonderful time. Occasionally, Grasshopper would see Ant at work.

"Poor Ant," he would say.

"You've got it all wrong! You're wasting these glorious summer days."

Ant took no notice.

He was too intent on gathering
food for the cold months to come.
The weather changed slowly at first.
The warmth left the air. It turned
sharper and grew chill at its heart.
It ripped the leaves from the trees
and, as the months rolled on,
it whistled and stung with cold.
    Ant lay deep down in the earth,
snug in his nest, surrounded by tasty corn.
Above him, on the wintry ground, Grasshopper tried to find
    shelter under a pile of leaves. He felt sick with cold
        and hunger, and as for his song…
            it would no longer come. He was too sad to sing.

        At the first sign of snow, Grasshopper knew
        his last days were near. As he watched the
            white flakes swirl from the sky, he closed
            his eyes and dreamed again of summer.
                Then it came to him…
                    "Ant!" he thought.
            "He must have plenty of food. Why, he did
            nothing but collect it all summer."

Grasshopper crept out from his pile
of leaves and stood at the entrance to Ant's nest.
"Help me, Ant! Help me, please!" he cried.
"I'm starving out here in the cold."

Deep down in the warm ground, Ant heard the
Grasshopper's call. He climbed to the top of his nest and poked
out his head. "Why should I help you?" he said.
"You laughed at me all summer.
It's your fault you don't have
any food."

"I know, I know,"
said Grasshopper. "If only
I'd been more like you."

"It's too late for that
now," snapped Ant, turning back to
go inside. But then he took one last look
at Grasshopper, shivering in the snow, and sighed.
"Oh very well," he said at last. "You can come inside."

The next summer, Grasshopper sang again to his heart's
content... but as he sang, he worked.
"What are you doing?" chirruped the other
grasshoppers. "Collecting food for winter? Who cares about
winter? Come and sing and leap around with us."
But Grasshopper shook his head.
He knew better now.

The Rat who was to Marry the Sun

Once upon a time, in a farmhouse surrounded by rice fields, lived two rich and happy rats. They only had one child – a dainty little daughter, with shiny fur, upright ears and glistening black eyes. The two rats wanted only the very best for their daughter. Day in and day out, they planned a magnificent future for her.

When Mother Rat saw her daughter was ready to be married, she scurried off to her husband, breathless with excitement. "The day has come!" she cried. "We must find our daughter a great and powerful husband."

"Of course," said Father Rat. "I shall summon the Sun immediately – for who is greater than the Sun?"

So Father Rat summoned the Sun, who appeared
without delay. "Little rat," said the Sun, "why do you
call for me?"

"Here stands my daughter," replied Father Rat.
"If she will have you, you may take her as your wife."

Then Father Rat turned to his daughter.
"Does this one please you, the Sun God
who lights up the world?" he asked.

"Father, he is too hot,"
said the little rat daughter.
"I do not want him.
Summon a better one!"

Hearing this, Father Rat
spoke again to the Sun.

"Great Sun God, is there a
being more powerful than you?"

"There is indeed," replied the Sun.
"When I want to shine on the earth, a cloud often comes by
and covers me up. My rays cannot break through it or
frighten it away. I am weaker than the Cloud."

The rats saw that this was so, and they summoned
a great cloud to come to them.

"Would you like to marry this Cloud?" asked Father Rat.

"Oh no Father," said the little rat daughter, shivering beneath her glossy fur. "He is dark and cold. Find me another powerful husband."

So Father Rat called out to the Cloud, "Listen, Great Cloud! Is there anyone more powerful than you?"

"I can cover up the Sun," replied the Cloud. "But I am powerless against the Wind. When he begins to blow, I am scattered into a thousand pieces."

The rats saw that this was so, and they summoned the Wind to come to them. He arrived with a

WHOOSH and a ROAR.

"Does the Wind please you as a husband?" shouted Mother Rat, her voice fighting the Wind's blustery gale.

"I don't like him at all," declared the little rat daughter. "He blows this way, then that – I'm worried I'll be blown right away. Find me a better husband than this!"

"Great Wind!" called Mother Rat. "Is there anyone more powerful than you?"

"I have the power to scatter clouds into a thousand pieces," roared the Wind. "But the Mountain is more powerful than I. However strong I am, he stands still against me. I can neither blow through him nor move him."

The rats saw that this was so, and they set out on a journey to the greatest mountain.

After many days' travel and with weary little feet, they arrived at the foot of the Great Mountain.

"Daughter," said Father Rat, when he had gained his breath. "Would you like this Mountain for a husband?"

"Oh no, Father," said the little rat daughter. "Look how hard and stony he is. I won't marry the Mountain. I won't!"

"King of the Mountains," cried Father Rat. "Is there anyone more powerful than you?"

"I can withstand the Wind," said the Mountain. "He cannot blow through me nor move me. But the rats are more powerful than I, for they can tunnel through me and make holes in me and there is nothing I can do."

The rats saw that this was so. They returned home and found their daughter the sleekest and most handsome of rats.

"Daughter," said Mother Rat.

"Does this fine young rat please you?"

Seeing him, the little rat daughter's eyes twinkled and glistened, making her more beautiful than ever.

"He is of my own kind," she thought.

"Mother, Father," she said, "I will have him. You may give me to him as a wife."

So the two rats were married and lived happily ever after. And the little rat's parents, who had once wanted their daughter to marry the Sun, shared in her happiness.

The Bird King

Once upon a time, the birds held a contest to see who was the greatest of them all.

"Whichever bird can fly the highest will be crowned king," said the Eagle, puffing out his golden feathers as he spoke.

"We will begin tomorrow at dawn."

The next morning, all the birds of the moors and mountains, of the forests and streams, gathered together to see who could fly the highest.

With a drum roll from the Woodpecker, hammering his beak against a tree, the birds were off. There was a flurry of feathers and furious whirring wings, as hundreds of birds shot up into the sky.

The first to turn back was
the Grouse, his heavy body too
much for his stumpy wings.

"Go-back, go-back, go-back," he called,
diving to the ground.

One bird after another grew tired and turned
around. Soon, only two could be seen in the sky –
the mighty Eagle and the tiny Wren.

The Wren flew straight up, while the Eagle soared in
great circles, higher and higher and higher.

"I can't... go... on," thought the Wren. At that moment
the Eagle passed him, and he flopped,
exhausted, onto the Eagle's back.

At last the Eagle, too, grew tired. He looked around the
airy blue and saw he was all alone. "I've won!" he cried.

"I'm the King! I'm the King!"

"Oh no you're not," said the Wren, flying above him.
"I'm higher than you!"

There was nothing the Eagle could do. He stretched out
his aching wings and glided to the ground.

And so that very day, in a ceremony
attended by all the birds, the tiny Wren
was crowned the Bird King.

The Wise Boar

It was springtime in Japan and the cherry trees were in blossom. Their branches were bowed down with foaming petals, and everyone flooded out from their houses to see the beautiful pink and white flowers. It was a time of laughter and singing and happiness for everyone...

except for the monkey-man.
All through the spring, he journeyed from village to village with his monkey, so it could perform to the jostling crowds. But no matter what he said, the monkey just sat there, unable to perform his tricks.

At last, the monkey-man
returned home, dragging
his monkey with him.

"I want you to call
for the butcher," he said to his
wife. "Ask him to come tomorrow
morning. This monkey's dancing days are
over. He's too old to be of any use to us. It's time I sold
him for meat so I can at least make some money out of him."

"Oh no," pleaded his wife. "Our monkey has served us all
his life. Let him live out his old age in comfort and peace."

"Quiet!" said the monkey-man.

"I have made up my mind."

In the next-door room, the monkey overheard every
word. "Oh dear me, oh dear me," he thought. "I'm to be
roasted and stewed! Beaten then eaten! What can I do? I'm too
old to go and live in the wild now." And as he sat and sighed
an idea came to him. "I've heard of a wild boar living in
the forest nearby. He is said to be very, very wise.

Perhaps he can help me?"

The next moment, the monkey slipped through the sliding door of the house and scampered away into the forest. He soon came to a clearing where he found the wise old boar, sniffing and snuffling for roots to eat.

With tears streaming down his face, the monkey told his woeful tale. "Oh great master," he said, bowing before the boar, "I have heard you are a wise animal. Can you help me in my time of trouble?"

Flattered by the monkey's talk, the boar decided to help him. "Your master has a child, does he not?" he asked.

The monkey nodded.

"I've seen the baby on the porch," the boar went on. "Tomorrow morning, when your master's wife lays down her baby on the floor, I shall come rushing up to the house and run off with it between my jaws."

"No!" the monkey gasped.

"Oh yes!" said the boar.
"And you shall come running
after me and save the baby.
Then, when the butcher comes for you,
neither the master nor his wife will
want to part with you. You'll see."

The monkey agreed to the plan,
but that night he barely slept, he was
so worried about his fate. As the first
rooster crowed in the dawn, the monkey
sprang up, just in time to see his master's
wife lay her child out on the porch. The next
instant, there was a scuffling sound and the
boar appeared, his white tusks glinting in
the morning sun. He scooped up the
child in his jaws and was off...

"Come back!" screamed the
master's wife. She ran to wake her
husband, but by the time he had
stumbled to the door, the boar
was no more than a brown blur
in the distance, heading for
the forested hills.

Behind him came the monkey, swinging from tree to tree, then dropping to the ground and bounding along on all fours, as if his life depended on it. Not long after, the monkey returned with the child in his arms.

As the master's wife cradled her baby to her she said, "Didn't I tell you, husband? We should never kill our monkey. If he hadn't been here, we would have lost our child forever."

"For once wife, you are right," said the monkey's master. "When the butcher comes you may send him away."

And for the rest of his life, the monkey was petted and pampered to his heart's delight.

The Boastful Crow

A sooty black crow stood alone on a sandy beach, his beady eyes on the lookout for food. It wasn't long before he heard a HONK-HONK

and a whirring of wings.

The next moment a flock of geese blotted out the sun as they noisily flapped down from the sky.

The crow watched them with his beak stuck haughtily in the air. "How clumsy you are!" he told them, as they crashed down beside him. "I've been watching you and laughing. All you do is go flap-flap-flap. Can you glide? Can you do somersaults in the air? Pah! I don't think so!"

The largest of the geese waddled up
to the crow until they were beak to beak.

"Let's have a flying competition
then," the goose declared.

"Yes!" squawked the crow.
"I'll show you what flying really is."

The crow set off right away, with all
the geese looking on. He soared straight into the
air, flying up and up and up. "I'll show them!"
he thought. He flew in circles, swooped
down like an arrow then
shot up again.

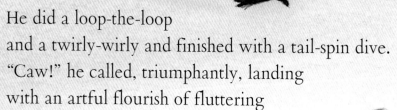

He did a loop-the-loop
and a twirly-wirly and finished with a tail-spin dive.
"Caw!" he called, triumphantly, landing
with an artful flourish of fluttering
wings. "Beat that!"

"I will!" said the goose. He launched himself into
the air and began flying over the sea. The crow flew after him.
"Just as I thought," called the crow.
"All you can do is flap-flap-flap."
On and on they flew, until water stretched out on all
sides and dry land was left far behind. After a little while,
the crow stopped taunting the goose. It was all he could do to
keep up with him. His aching wings begged for rest and he
looked with fear at the churning water below.

The goose watched the crow and smiled to himself.
"Why do you keep touching the water?" he asked. "Is it another
of your flying tricks?"

"No!" cried the crow, all pride gone. "I can't…last…
much longer. If you don't help me, I'll drown!"

"Do you promise never to boast again?"

"I promise," gasped the crow and flopped, exhausted,
onto the goose's back.

The goose beat his powerful wings and together
they turned back to the shore.

"Ah!" sighed the crow. "Flap-flap-flap!
What a perfect way to fly."

The Bear Son

In a land far away to the north, where the ground is thick with snow, a little old woman lived by the shores of a frozen sea.

She was poor and had little to eat, but she had sealskin clothes to keep her warm, and the hunters of the village always gave her a share of their meat. One winter's day at dusk, a hunter stopped by the old woman's hut.

"We've killed one of the nanoq – a big white bear," he said, handing her a hunk of meat.

In his other arm, the hunter held a cub.

"Do you want him too?" the hunter asked.

"He'll die if we leave him outside, now that his mother is dead."

"What would I want with a cub?" asked the woman.

"He could be company for you, on a winter's night," the hunter replied.

Just then, the bear cub opened his berry-black eyes, and the old woman held out her hands for him, and took him inside.

She settled him by the fire for warmth, for he was frozen through. And when he stirred, she gave him melted blubber to drink and scraps of seal meat to eat.

That night, she went to sleep with the cub beside her, curled up in a snow-white ball.

The old woman talked to her cub every day, until he could understand human speech. He would sniff her whenever he wanted food, and when the village children came to play, she would say,

"Remember, little nanoq, you must put your claws away."

And he did.

But after a while the bear grew too strong to play with the children. One flick from his great white paws was enough to break their toys or push them over. So the men played with the bear instead. They wrestled and tussled and rode on his back, and the bear grew stronger and stronger.

That winter, the men looked at the bear and said, "We call him little nanoq, but this bear is as big as an iceberg. Let us take him with us when we go hunting. He may help us catch seals."

When she heard this, the old woman wove her bear a thick collar. "Now everyone will know you are mine," she said. "And they will know you are not to be harmed."

At dawn the next day,
the hunters came to her door.
"Little nanoq," they called,
"come out and earn a share of
our catch. Come hunting with us,
little nanoq."
  At dusk, the hunters returned.
"Your bear is stronger than the
strongest hunter. He is bigger than
any bear ever seen. By hunting with
him, we have caught many seals."
  And the old woman
smiled with pride.

After that, the bear went out hunting on the ice
each winter, and caught seals as they came up to
breathe. In summer he crept up
on the seals as they slept.

And when he returned, he and the
old woman would share his catch. They would sit
together in the door of her hut, and the old woman
would point to the shining stars.

"There is the Great Bear," the old woman said.
"Like you, he fell into the hands of men. And when he died,
he became wonderfully bright, and rose up as stars
in the sky."

The people in the other villages came to know the bear.
Although they sometimes came close to catching him,
they always let him go when they saw his collar.
"We mustn't kill that bear," they said to each other.
"The old woman needs his help. She is the bear's foster
mother, and he is her son."

89

But then came a new band of hunters from beyond the mountains. They heard of the bear who must not be killed, and the chief hunter said, "Of all the animals we hunt, the nanoq is the most prized. And this is the greatest nanoq of them all. If I ever see that bear, I will kill it."

When the old woman heard this, she wept, for she knew what she had to do. "You can't stay here with me, little nanoq," she said. "If you stay among men you will die."

And the bear thrust its muzzle right down onto the floor and wept too, it made him so sad to leave her.

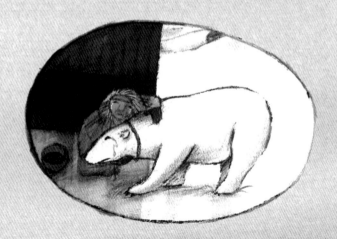

The old woman kept the bear by her side all that winter, while the snow fell in blizzards outside. "You must not go out now, little nanoq," she said. "For now is the time for bear hunting, and you are the greatest prize."

She waited until the frost melted in the sun, and the sky was clear of clouds. Then she said, "It is time for you to leave. Travel north, across the sea of ice.

There you will find your own kind."

The bear turned to go, but the old woman cried for him to stop. "I need to know if he's going to make it. I need to know if he's going to live," she thought.

And she dipped her hand in oil and smeared it in soot. Then she stroked her hand along his side, leaving a broad black streak. The bear looked at her one last time and padded away, across the sea of ice.

Spring turned into summer. The ground was no longer white, but bright with flowers. Geese flew overhead, berries ripened and young birds took to the air. And every time hunters passed through the village, the old woman asked, "Have you seen a great white bear, with a broad black streak on his side?"

When they shook their heads, the old woman sighed.

Then, at last, as the waters began to freeze again, hunters came from the far north, with tales of a great white bear, as big as an iceberg, with a broad black streak on his side.

"So he is alive," said the old woman. And in the long winter evenings, the old woman looked up at the stars, at the Great Bear in the sky.

And she thought of her bear, living far away, and smiled.

The Battle of the Crabs

Once upon a time, on an island in the Sulu Sea,
the fiddler crabs came together for a meeting.
One of them waved his great claw in the air and said,
"What shall we do about the waves? They sing so loudly,
all day and all night, that we cannot possibly sleep."

"There is only one answer!" said the oldest crab.

"We must fight them."

So the crabs said goodbye to their wives and scuttled
out from their mudhole homes to line up on the shore
in a great long row.

"What are you doing?" asked the sea turtles, watching
them from the sandy banks. "It's high tide! Get back in your
burrows or you'll be washed away by the waves."

"Nonsense," said the crabs. "This is war and we're going to win." So saying, they raised their claws at the ocean and as the waves rose up to meet them... they charged.

But their snapping pincers were powerless against the swell of the sea. The foam alone scattered the crabs across the sand, then the waves sucked them back and carried them away - far, far away - out into the open ocean.

As the sun slipped down the sky and lit the water with a fiery glow, the wives of the crabs began to worry. "Whatever has happened to our husbands?" they asked, poking out of their burrows. "Why haven't they come back from battle?" They scuttled down to the shore in search of the missing men. But no sooner had they arrived than the waves came crashing down again, and took the wives the way of their husbands.

The sea turtles shook their heads sadly. "What fools they were," they said, "to battle with the waves."

For a long time, no crabs could be seen on the
shores of the Sulu Sea and the mudhole homes
were empty. Until...

one day, at high tide, thousands of
little crabs came scuttling out of the
sea. They ran up the beach as fast
as their eight legs could take them.

The sea turtles watched with
wonder. For it seemed as if these little
crabs knew what had happened to their
kind before. Every day they would rush down
to the water's edge, ready to fight the waves.
Then, their courage would fail them and they'd
rush back up the beach again.

They can still be seen today... running to and fro...
caught between the soft, safe sand and the surging, singing sea.